To Noah and Yona (with thanks to Carter, Gavi, Lev, Quinlan, and Stellan).
And in solidarity with HarperCollins's union members. —J.R.

To Doris, my lovely wife, for believing in me —E.M.

Clarion Books is an imprint of HarperCollins Publishers.

Turbo's Special Delivery
Text copyright © 2023 by Jean Reagan
Illustrations copyright © 2023 by Eduardo Marticorena

Library of Congress Control Number: 2022045232
ISBN 978-0-06-328893-5

The illustrations in this book were created with the artist's trusty Wacom Cintiq.
Design by Phil Caminiti
23 24 25 26 27   RTLO   10 9 8 7 6 5 4 3 2 1

First Edition

TURBO'S
SPECIAL DELIVERY

WRITTEN BY
JEAN REAGAN

ILLUSTRATED BY
EDUARDO MARTICORENA

Clarion Books
An Imprint of HarperCollinsPublishers

Turbo Truck was fast.

VERY fast.

Heavy loads?
Treacherous routes?
Faraway destinations?

No problem!

He zoomed along—zigging and zagging—even on bumpy, curvy roads.

When he got back, he always heard:

"TOOT-TOOT!
Hooray!"

"BEEP-BEEP!
So fast!"

"HONK-HONK!
Good job, Turbo!"

Turbo beamed.
He loved *FAST*.
But SLOW?
Booooooooring.

Luckily, someone always needed a super-speedy delivery.

Until one day, every truck got a job . . .

except Turbo.

All morning, he wandered the warehouse, paced the perimeter, and roamed around the ramps.

At last Rosa, the supervisor, shouted,

"SPECIAL DELIVERY!"

"Sorry, Turbo," she said. "This load is fragile.
And everyone knows you only have one speed—*fast*."

He scooted closer.
"Do you think you can do it?"
Rosa asked.

Turbo honked a confident **BEEP-BEEP-BEEP.**
Sure I can. But even he worried, *Can I?*

"Okay—here's the deal," Rosa said.
"Deliver to Pleasant Valley Park."

"Remember, this is a *special* delivery.
No zigging. No zagging. No tilting, bouncing, or sliding."

Turbo wondered, *What could be so special?*

VROOOOM! He zoomed out of the lot.

Ooooops! His load began to slide.

He gently tapped the brakes.

SQUE-EEEEE-EEEEEEE-EEEEEAK.

The load stopped sliding.
Whew.
Okay—slow.

At a bump he *usually* flew right over, Turbo E-E-E-E-EASED up one side and down the other.

At the zigs, he Z-I-I-I-I-I-I-I-I-GGED.

At the zags, he Z-A-A-A-A-A-A-A-GGED.

Vehicles zipped by.

Passing him!

Turbo sped up.

But then he remembered Rosa's warnings—
and slowed back down.

Good thing, because around the bend . . .

. . . a family of ducks waddled into the road.

Did Turbo screech to a stop?

Swerve around the ducks?

Smash his precious cargo?

No! He went from *slow* motion to *no* motion.

The lake glistened. The ducks quacked,

THANKS!

THANKS!

THANKS!

When Turbo got back to the route,
he noticed—for the first time ever—
the fresh mountain air tickling his windshield
and the wild colors reflected in his mirrors.

Finally, he crested the last hill.
Far, far below was Pleasant Valley Park.

The road dropped. Steep and curvy.

YEEHAW!

HONK! HONK! HONK!

WHEEEEEEEEE!

*Wait. Wait. No.
I can't mess
up now.*

Instead,
Turbo checked his brakes.
One. Two. Three times—just to be sure.

He turned on his flashers
and started creeeeeeping

DOWN . . .

DOWN . . .

DOWN.

At last—he rolled into the park. And honked lightly.

Turbo held his breath as they opened his doors. Inside was a . . .

. . . perfect cake!

Everyone cheered.

Turbo's engine purred
with pride.

After the party, he drove back

fast,

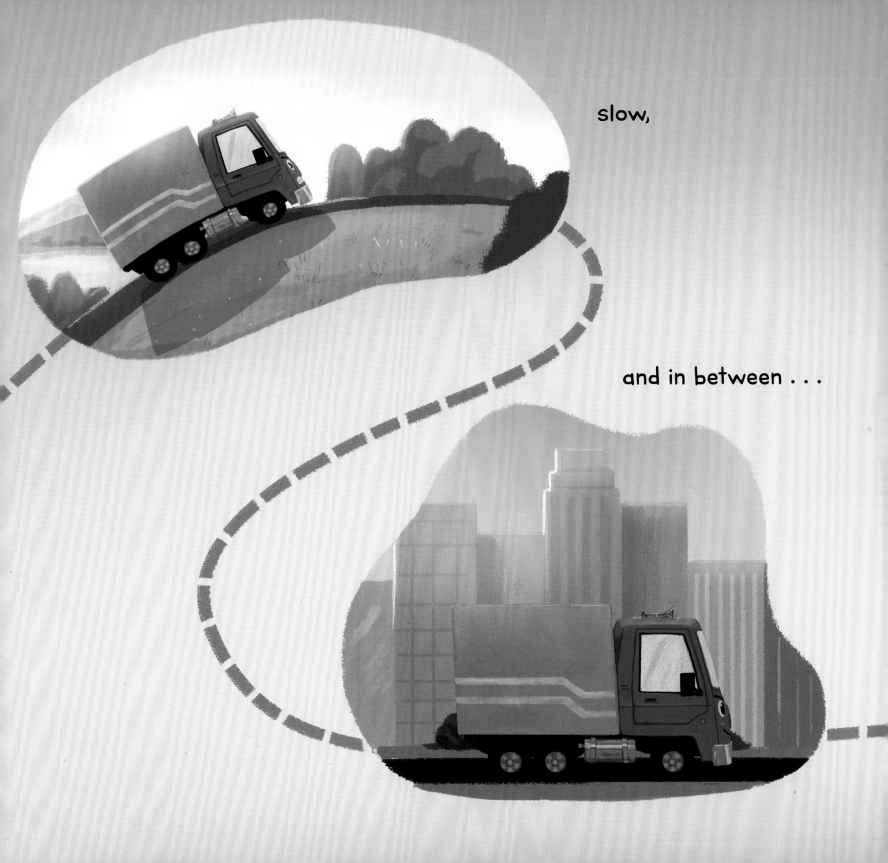

slow,

and in between . . .

. . . and pulled into the lot.

No
"TOOT-TOOT!"
"BEEP-BEEP!"
"HONK-HONK!"

Everyone was already tucked in
for the night. But Turbo still beamed.

He turned off his engine and shut off his lights.

GOOD JOB, TURBO!